My First Experience

Going to the Doctor

Written by Catherine Mackenzie
Illustrated by Lynn Breeze
Published by Christian Focus Publications

Strut the chicken is hiding in every picture in this book.
Can you find him?

My name is Marty. I am visiting my friend Tina and her Grandpa, Grandpa Jack. Mum has asked Grandpa Jack to look after me today. She has to go off to work.

Tina is pretending to be a nurse. But Tina stops playing and says she doesn't feel well. Grandpa Jack says we should take Tina to see the doctor. I ask Jesus to make Tina better.

Hear, O Lord and answer me, for I am poor and needy. Guard my life. I love you. I trust you. Psalm 86:1-2

We put on warm clothes. Then we get in a bus and go to visit the doctor who works in a building called a surgery. Tina is feeling sad. She has never been to the doctor's before. Will it be a nice place?

When we arrive a friendly man shows us where the waiting room is. We then wait until the doctor is ready to see us. Tina reads a comic and I play with some toys. The doctor's surgery is a nice place.

God gives strength to the weary.
Isaiah 40:29

Tina and I wonder what the doctor will be like. Will she be friendly? We don't know. But Jesus knows everything. He knows where we are and what we are doing. I tell Tina that Jesus loves her and she smiles.

Soon the doctor comes in and says, 'Tina Jack to Dr. Singh's surgery please.' Grandpa Jack waves at the doctor. The doctor smiles and takes us to her room .

Cast your cares on the Lord.
Psalm 55:22

There are lots of interesting things to see in the doctor's room. There is a big desk with papers on it. There are cupboards and drawers full of medicines and pills. Are we allowed to touch them?

In the corner there is a first aid kit with bandages and creams and other bits and pieces inside. We are not allowed to touch any of these things in the doctor's room. They belong to the doctor.

He who obeys instructions guards his life. Proverbs 19:16

The doctor shows me her stethoscope and how you are supposed to wear them in your ears. She then lets me listen to Tina's heart beat. It makes a thumpedy thump noise. What will the doctor do next with the stethoscope?

The doctor takes her stethoscope and places it against Tina's back. She listens carefully as Tina breathes in and out. Then she looks at Tina's tongue and all the way down her throat. Tina says her throat is sore and she cries a little. I give Tina a hug. That makes her smile.

Be strong and do not give up.
2 Chronicles 15:7

The doctor gives Grandpa Jack a piece of paper with writing on it. This is called a prescription.

We take the prescription to the chemist and give it to the pharmacist. What will the pharmacist do with the prescription?

When we arrive at the chemist, the pharmacist takes the prescription and gives Grandpa Jack a bottle with bright red liquid in it. Tina has to take one spoonful three times a day. This will make her better.

I am the Lord who heals you.
Exodus 15:26

When we get back to Tina's house my mum is back from work. Grandpa shows her Tina's medicine. I tell her all about our visit to the doctor.

Later I tell mum how I helped Tina and told her about Jesus. Mum is pleased with me.

Mum and I pray to Jesus before I go to sleep. I thank Jesus for my friend Tina and for her red medicine. Mum asks God to make Tina all better.

The Lord cares for those who trust in him. Nahum 1:7

You can also speak to
Jesus anytime you like.

Dear Jesus

Thank you for loving me. Thank you for looking after me.

Thank you for doctors and nurses and all the people
who work hard to make me feel better. Please look after
me and all the people that I love.

You are lovely Jesus. When I ask you to be my friend you
will always be with me. You will never leave me.

Amen.